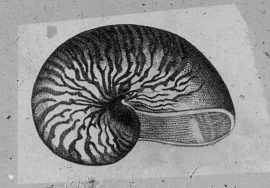

Western Heroes Vol II

COWBOY
& Octopus

JON SCIESZKA
& LANE SMITH

Viking

VIKING
Published by Penguin Group
Penguin Young Readers Group, 345 Hudson Street,
New York, New York 10014, U.S.A.
Penguin Group (Canada), 90 Eglinton Avenue East, Suite 700,
Toronto,
Ontario, Canada M4P 2Y3 (a division of Pearson Penguin Canada Inc.)

Penguin Books Ltd, Registered Offices: 80 Strand, London WC2R 0RL, England

First published in 2007 by Viking, a division of Penguin Young Readers Group

1 3 5 7 9 10 8 6 4 2

LIBRARY OF CONGRESS CATALOGING-IN-PUBLICATION DATA
Scieszka, Jon.
Cowboy and Octopus / by Jon Scieszka and Lane Smith.
p. cm.
Summary: Although Cowboy and Octopus have different opinions
about beans and knock-knock jokes, their friendship endures.
ISBN 978-0-670-91058-8 (hardcover)
[1. Cowboys—Fiction. 2. Octopuses—Fiction. 3. Friendship—Fiction. 4. Humorous stories.] I. Smith, Lane, ill.
II. Title.
PZ7.S41267Co 2007
[Fic]-dc22
2007001561

Manufactured in China
Set in Arial Rounded

DESIGN BY
MOLLY LEACH

TO MY BEST PAL, OCTOPUS
—COWBOY

To my good friend, Cowboy
—Octopus

Cowboy meets Octopus

Cowboy is confused.
"This dang thing is always broke."

"Hello," says Octopus. "I think I can help.
You get on that side. I'll get on this side."

"Yee-haw!" says Cowboy. **"You fixed it."**

Octopus says, "Some things work better with a friend."

"You wanna be friends?" says Cowboy.

"Certainly," says Octopus.

So Cowboy and Octopus shake hands . . .
and shake hands, and shake hands,
and shake hands, and shake hands,
and shake hands, and shake hands,
and shake hands.

Octopus needs help.

So he calls his friend Cowboy.

"I have to hold all of this together . . .
then hammer this in," says Octopus.
"When I nod my head,
you hit it. Okay?"

"Sounds loco to me," says Cowboy.
"But okay."

Octopus holds everything together.

Octopus nods his head.

BAM! Cowboy hits it.

"Need any more help?"
says Cowboy.

"No," says Octopus.
"Sometimes help from a
friend isn't the best help."

Chow time

Cowboy decides to surprise
Octopus and make him dinner.

Octopus is definitely surprised.

"Heavens," says Octopus.
"What is this?"

"I cooked all my favorites just for you,"
says Cowboy. "Beans and Bacon,
Bacon and Beans, and just plain
Beans…with a little bit of bacon."

"Oh my," says Octopus.

Octopus doesn't like beans.
He doesn't like bacon.

But he does like it that Cowboy has worked so hard just for him.

Octopus licks one bean.

"Mmm-mmm," says Octopus. "I am so full."

Cowboy smiles.
He is glad his friend likes his surprise.

"Wait till you see what's for dessert," says Cowboy.

Octopus says, "I'll bet I can guess."

"Do you like my Halloween costume?" says Octopus.

"What are you?" says Cowboy.

Octopus says, **"I am a shark."**

"Oh yeah," says Cowboy.
"Now I see your little shark thing."

"It's not very scary, is it?" says Octopus.

Cowboy says, "Nope."

"I'm going back to my first idea," says Octopus.

"**Whoa!** What the heck are you?"
says Cowboy.

Octopus says,
"I am the Tooth Fairy."

"Now that's scary," says Cowboy.

"**Very scary.**"

Beautiful DAY

"Isn't it a **BEAUTIFUL** day?"
says Octopus.

Cowboy says, "No, it ain't."

 WHO'S THERE?

"Knock knock," says Octopus.

Cowboy opens the door. "Nobody there."

"No, no," says Octopus.
"You say, 'Who's there?'"

"Ain't nobody there!" says Cowboy.

"I know," says Octopus. **"It's a joke."**

Cowboy thinks for a second.
"Well, dang. It's not a very funny joke."

Octopus laughs. "No, Cowboy. The joke comes after you say, 'Who's there?'"

"Okay," says Cowboy. **"Who's there?"**

Octopus says, "Lettuce."

"Lettuce?" says Cowboy.

"That's crazy talk.
Lettuce can't knock on a door."

Cowboy laughs.
"That is a great joke, Octopus."

Octopus laughs, too.

Telling Cowboy a knock knock
joke didn't work out so well.

But a lettuce knocking on
a door is pretty dang funny.

That's the TRUTH

"Do you like my new hat?" says Cowboy.

"**Wow,**" says Octopus. "That is really ... um ... different. Do you like my new hat?"

Cowboy says, "Nope."

"Hey!" says Octopus. "I said something nice to you. Why don't you say something nice to me? I thought we were friends."

"We are friends," says Cowboy. "And that's why I am telling you—your new hat looks like something my horse dropped behind him. **'Cause that's the truth.**"